W9-AZC-454

If You Give a Pig a Pancake

Once again, for Stephen —F.B.
For Laura Geringer, with love and eternal gratitude —L.N.

If You Give a

No part of this publication may be reproduced
in whole or in part, or stored in a retrieval system, or transmitted
in any form or by any means, electronic, mechanical, photocopying,
recording, or otherwise, without written permission of the publisher.
For information regarding permission, write to
HarperCollins Publishers, 10 East 53rd Street, New York, NY 10022.

ISBN 0-439-04223-2

Text copyright © 1998 by Laura Numeroff.
Illustrations copyright © 1998 by Felicia Bond.
All rights reserved.
Published by Scholastic Inc., 555 Broadway, New York, NY 10012,
by arrangement with HarperCollins Publishers.
SCHOLASTIC and associated logos are trademarks and/or registered
trademarks of Scholastic Inc.

12 11 10 9 8 7 6 5 4 3 2 1   8 9/9 0 1 2 3/0

Printed in the U.S.A.   36

First Scholastic printing, September 1998

Pig a Pancake

BY Laura Numeroff

ILLUSTRATED BY Felicia Bond

SCHOLASTIC INC.
New York   Toronto   London   Auckland   Sydney
Mexico City   New Delhi   Hong Kong

If you give a pig a pancake,

she'll want some syrup to go with it.

You'll give her some of your
favorite maple syrup.

She'll probably get all sticky,

so she'll want to take a bath.

She'll ask you for some bubbles.

When you give her the bubbles,
she'll probably ask you for a toy.
You'll have to find your rubber duck.

The duck will remind her of the farm where she was born.
She might feel homesick and want to visit her family.

She'll want you to come too.
She'll look through your closet
for a suitcase.

Then she'll look under your bed.

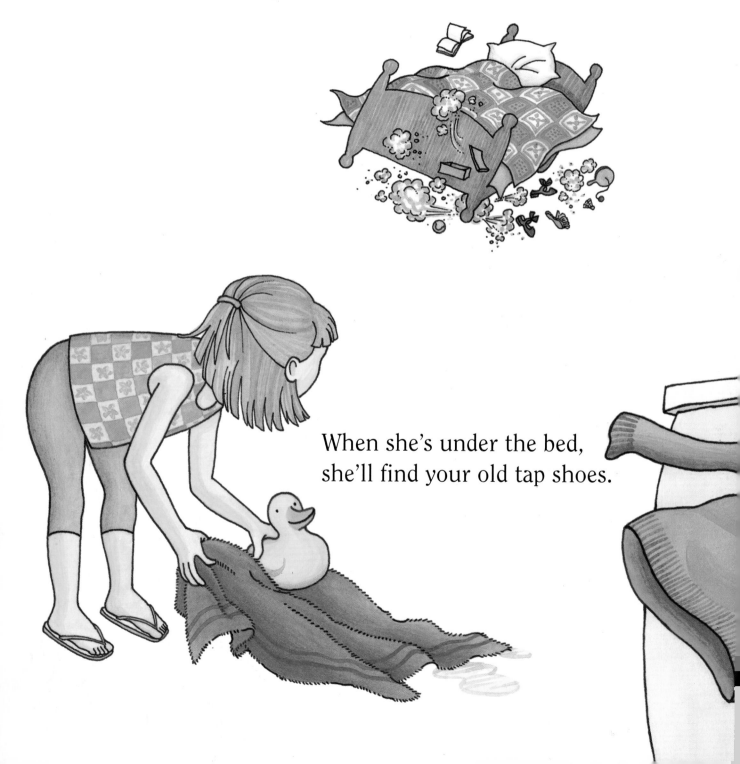

When she's under the bed,
she'll find your old tap shoes.

She'll try them on. She'll probably need something special to wear with them.

When she's all dressed, she'll ask for some music.

You'll play your
very best piano piece,
and she'll start dancing.

Then she'll want you to take her picture.

So you'll have to get your camera.

When she sees the picture,

she'll ask you to take more.

Then she'll want to send one to each of her friends.

You'll have to give her
some envelopes and stamps

and take her to the mailbox.

On the way, she'll see the tree in your backyard.
She'll want to build a tree house.

So you'll have to get her some wood,
a hammer, and some nails.

When the tree house is finished,

she'll want to decorate it.

She'll ask for wallpaper and glue.

When she hangs the wallpaper, she'll get all sticky.

Feeling sticky will remind her of your favorite maple syrup.

She'll probably ask you for some.

And chances are,

if she asks you for some syrup,

she'll want a pancake to go with it.